W9-CEP-124

Leo the Late Bloomer

BY ROBERT KRAUS • PICTURES BY JOSE ARUEGO

SCHOLASTIC INC.
New York Toronto London Auckland Sydney

For Ken Dewey
and
For Pamela, Bruce and Billy

No part of this publication may be reproduced in whole or in part, or stored in a retrieval system, or transmitted in any form or by any means, electronic, mechanical, photocopying, recording, or otherwise, without written permission of the publisher. For information regarding permission, write to HarperCollins Publishers, 10 East 53rd St., New York, NY 10022.

ISBN 0-590-51589-6

Text copyright © 1971 by Robert Kraus.
Illustrations copyright © 1971 by Jose Aruego.
All rights reserved. Published by Scholastic Inc., 555 Broadway, New York, NY 10012, by arrangement with HarperCollins Publishers.

SCHOLASTIC and associated logos are trademarks and/or registered trademarks of Scholastic Inc.

12 11 10 9 8 7 6 5 4 3 2   4 5 6 7 8/0

Printed in the U.S.A.   14

First Scholastic printing, September 1998

Leo couldn't do anything right.

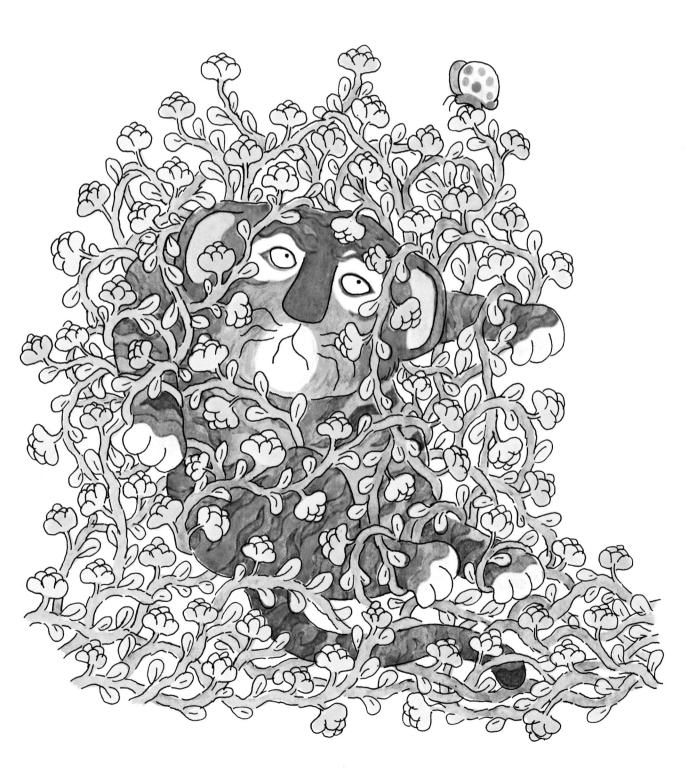

He couldn't read.

He couldn't write.

owl

Elephant

Snake

Plover

Crocodile

He couldn't draw.

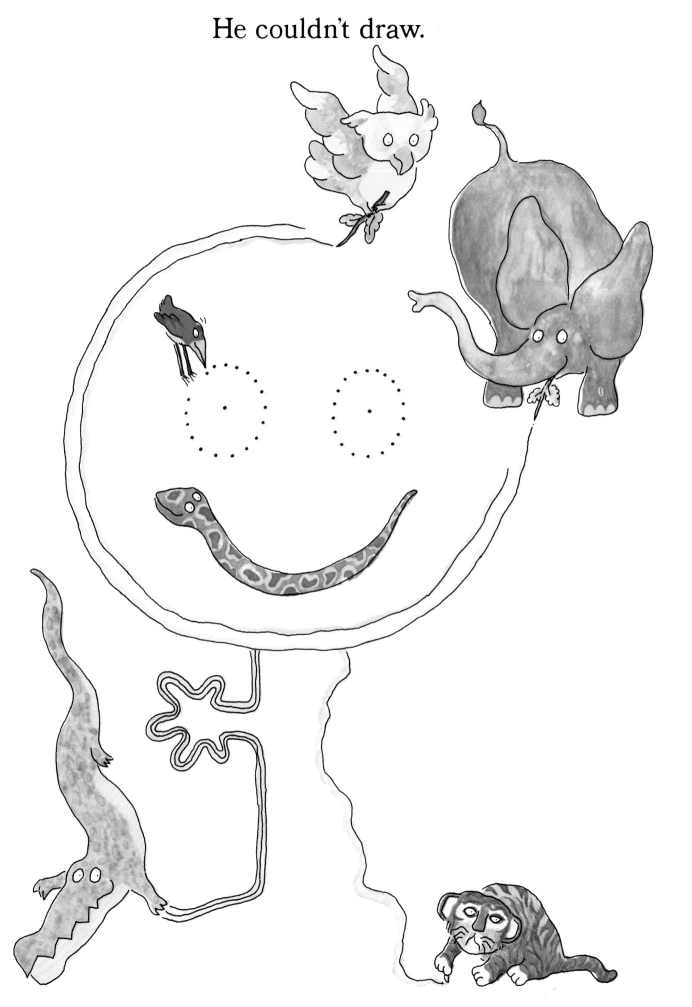

He was a sloppy eater.

And, he never said a word.

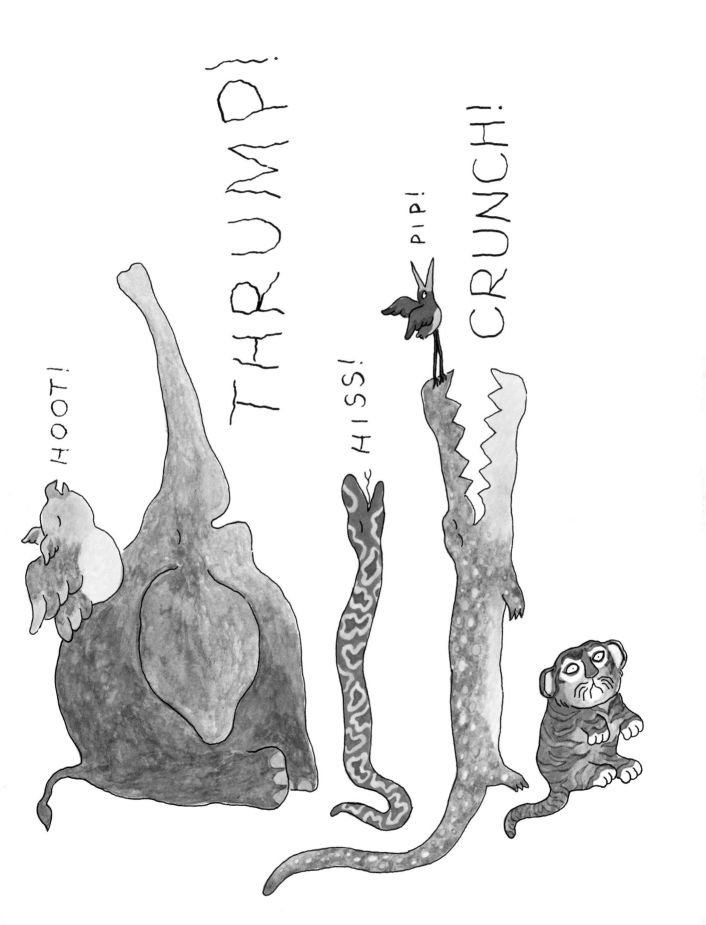

"What's the matter with Leo?"
asked Leo's father.
"Nothing," said Leo's mother.
"Leo is just a late bloomer."
"Better late than never," thought Leo's father.

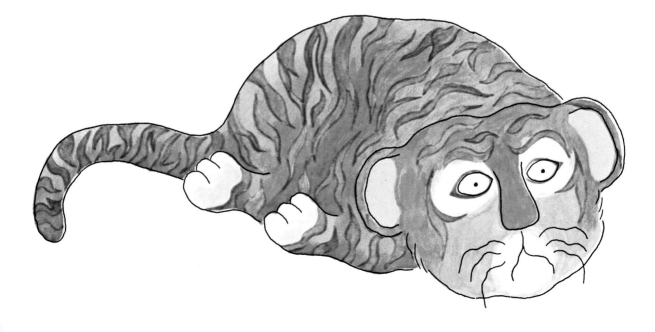

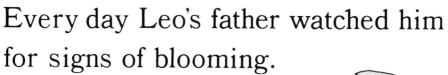

Every day Leo's father watched him
for signs of blooming.

And every night Leo's father watched him for signs of blooming.

"Are you sure Leo's a bloomer?"
asked Leo's father.
"Patience," said Leo's mother,
"A watched bloomer doesn't bloom."

So Leo's father watched television
instead of Leo.

The snows came.
Leo's father wasn't watching.
But Leo still wasn't blooming.

The trees budded.
Leo's father wasn't watching.
But Leo still wasn't blooming.

Then one day,
in his own good time,
Leo bloomed!

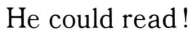

He could read!

He could write!

He could draw!

He ate neatly!

He also spoke.
And it wasn't just a word.
It was a whole sentence.
And that sentence was...

"I made it!"